AUSSIE BIG ACHIEVERS

CATHY FREEMAN

written by RICHARD SIMPKIN

illustrated by DEBRA O'HALLORAN

Other AUSSIE BIG ACHIEVERS books
STEVE IRWIN
ASH BARTY
SHANE WARNE

We acknowledge the Traditional Owners of the land on which we publish books, the Quandamooka people and pay our respects to Elders past, present and emerging.

Published by:
Boolarong Press,
38/1631 Wynnum Road
Tingalpa Qld 4173
Australia.
www.boolarongpress.com.au

First published 2021

A catalogue record for this book is available from the National Library of Australia

ISBN: 9781922643179 (Paperback)

Printed and bound by Watson Ferguson & Company, Tingalpa, Australia

DEDICATION

This book is dedicated to You,
because You can achieve any dream You have!

Cathy Freeman was born in Mackay Queensland on 16 February 1973.

Cathy's mum and step dad knew that she enjoyed running and they encouraged her to do so. Cathy's step dad told her to put up a sign in their house that said, "I am the world's greatest athlete". The sign helped Cathy believe in herself and believe that one day she would be the world's greatest athlete.

I am the World's greatest athlete

When Cathy was just eight she won her first gold medal at the school athletics carnival.

Cathy continued to win many running races and when she was 17 Cathy was selected in the Australian Commonwealth Games team. She won a gold medal in the 4 x 100 metre relay race, making Cathy the first female Aboriginal to win a gold medal at the Commonwealth Games in athletics.

In 1990, Cathy was named Young Australian of the Year.

Cathy was not just an incredible athlete, she was also an inspiration to children throughout Australia. At a young age Cathy was showing all of us that if you believe in yourself then you can achieve anything.

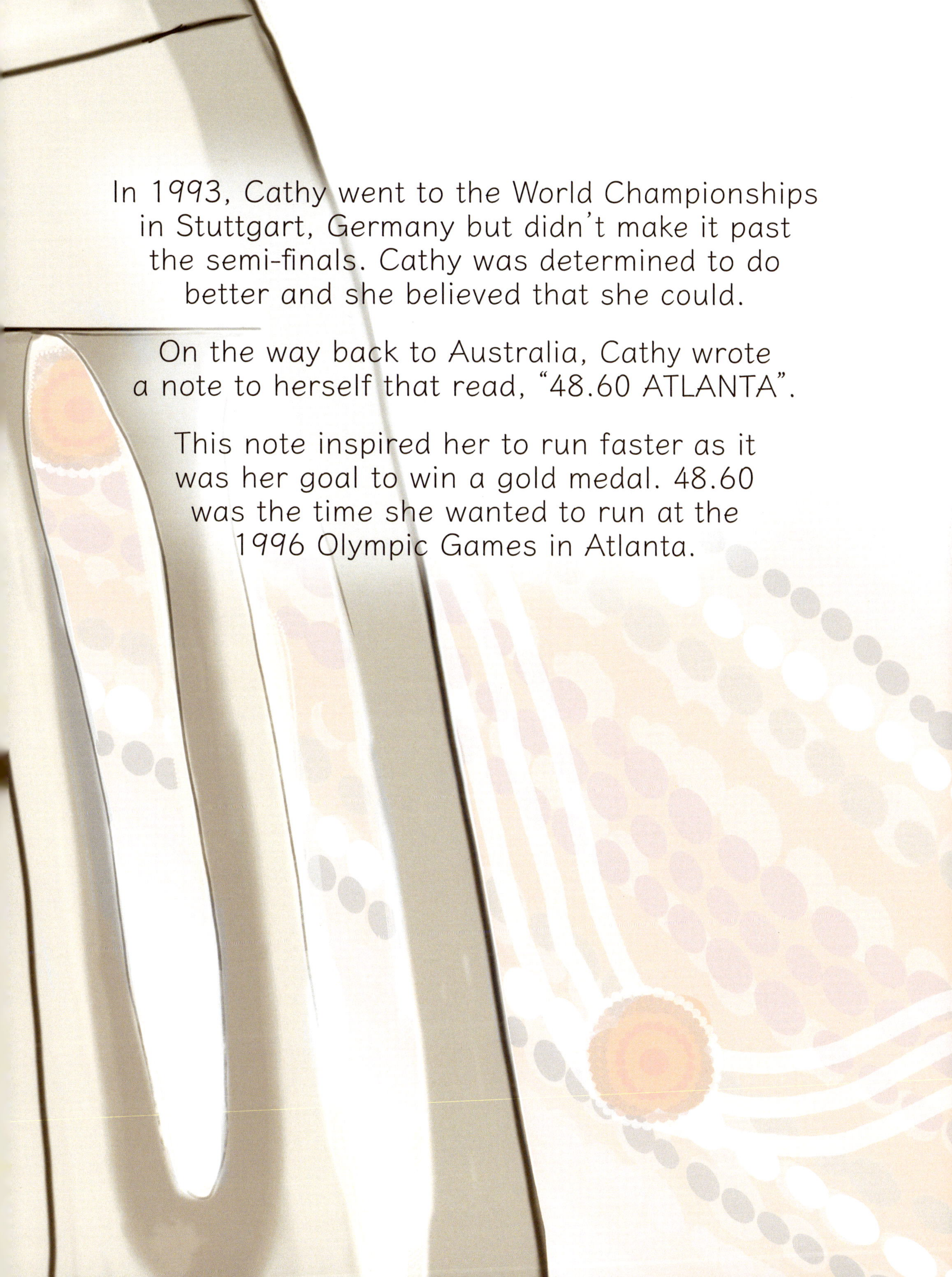

In 1993, Cathy went to the World Championships in Stuttgart, Germany but didn't make it past the semi-finals. Cathy was determined to do better and she believed that she could.

On the way back to Australia, Cathy wrote a note to herself that read, "48.60 ATLANTA".

This note inspired her to run faster as it was her goal to win a gold medal. 48.60 was the time she wanted to run at the 1996 Olympic Games in Atlanta.

The next year at the 1994 Commonwealth Games, Cathy won both the 200 and 400 metre gold medals. After she won the two races Cathy put both the Aboriginal and Australian flags around her to show that she was a proud Aboriginal Australian who represented all Australians.

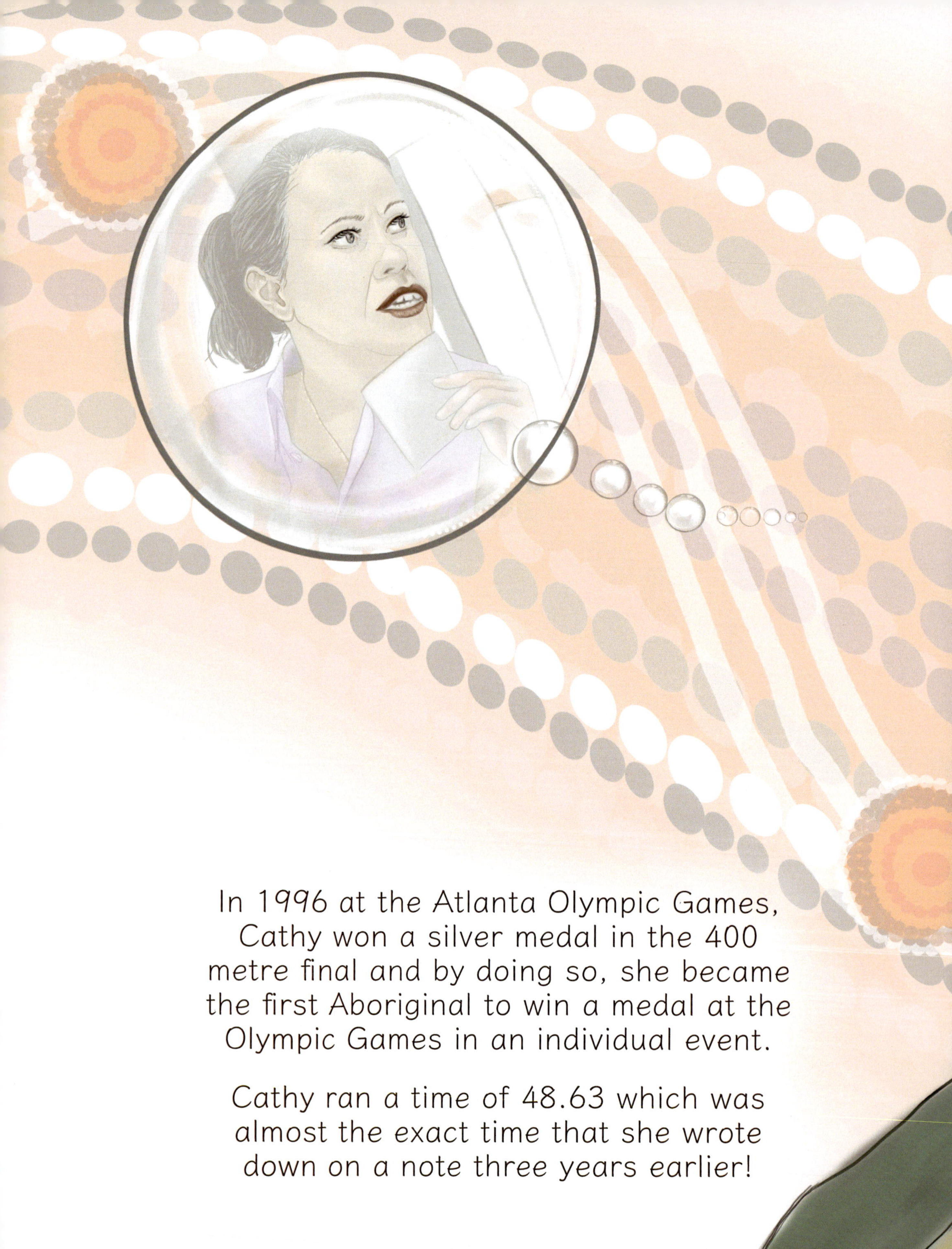

In 1996 at the Atlanta Olympic Games, Cathy won a silver medal in the 400 metre final and by doing so, she became the first Aboriginal to win a medal at the Olympic Games in an individual event.

Cathy ran a time of 48.63 which was almost the exact time that she wrote down on a note three years earlier!

CENTENNIAL OLYMPIC GAMES
Atlanta 1976

Ever since Cathy was a little girl; it was her dream to win a gold medal at an Olympic Games.

Cathy knew that if she wanted to be the best in the world, she would have to train very hard, believe in herself, persevere and to dream big.

But could Cathy make her dream come true?

From 1996 until 2000 Cathy won 41 out of 42 races, the only one that she didn't win was due to injury. She was considered the fastest female runner for 400 metres in the world, but what Cathy really wanted was to win a gold medal at the Sydney Olympic Games.

1998
1999

In 1998 Cathy was named Australian of the Year making history again by being the only person to be the young Australian of the year (in 1990) and the Australian of the year.

Cathy was not only representing herself, but she was representing her people who are the First Nations people of Australia.

At the Sydney Olympic Games in 2000, Cathy was chosen from the entire Australian Olympic team to light the flame in the stadium which announced to the world that the The Games had begun.

By doing so Cathy was representing all Australians and inspired a generation of Aboriginal and non-Aboriginal children to follow their dreams, no matter how big or small.

SYDNEY 2000

At the Sydney Olympic Games, Cathy was the favourite to win the gold medal in the women's 400 metre final and the whole of Australia, if not the world were hoping that Cathy could win the gold.

On Monday 25 September 2000, Cathy walked onto the track for the women's 400 metre final. There were over 110,000 people in the stadium screaming her name.

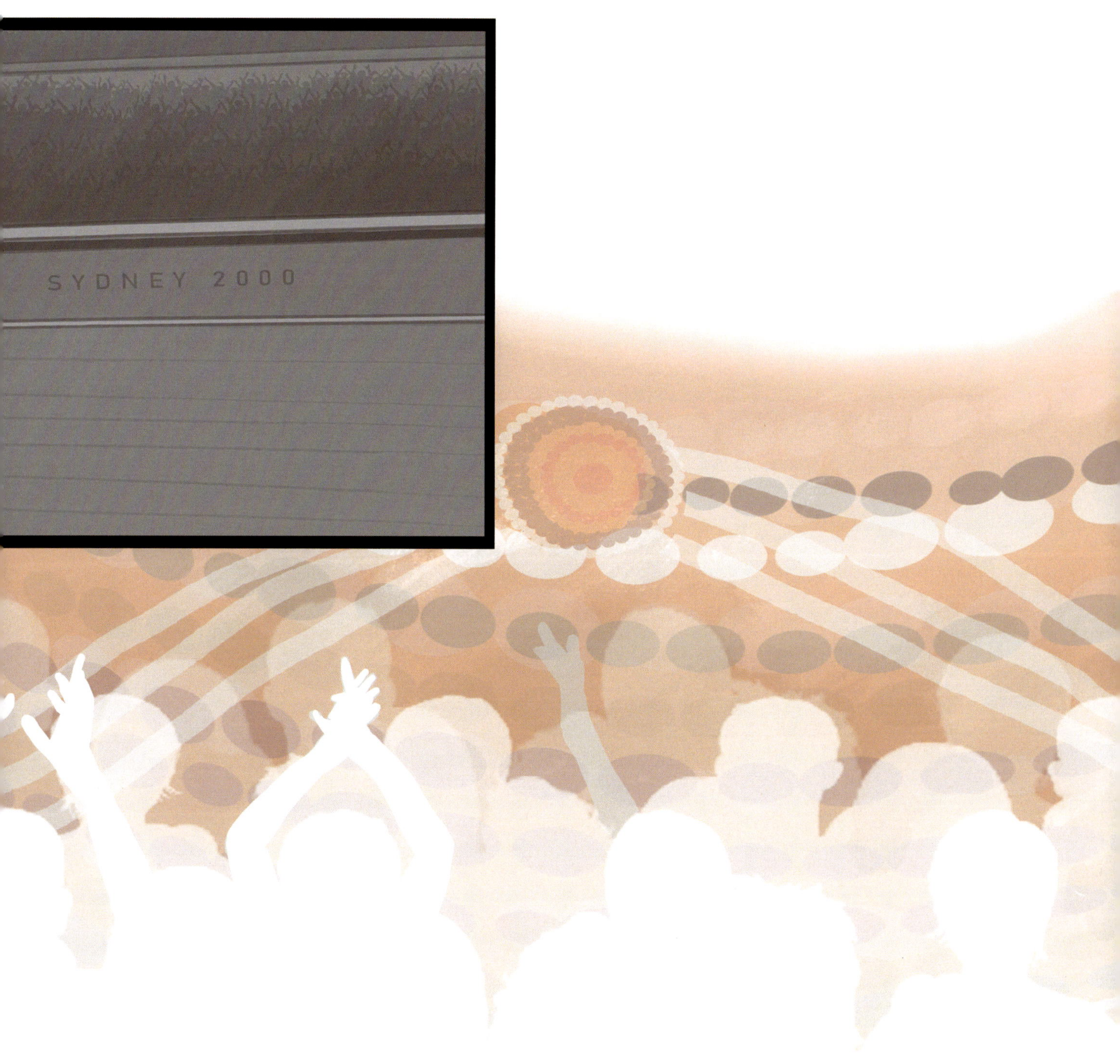

Everyone in the packed stadium wanted Cathy to win. There were also billions of people watching the race around the world on TV. Could Cathy win the Gold medal?

Ready, Set, Go and the race started. Cathy had trained for this race since she was a little girl.

She had dreamed her whole life about this race. Cathy had to believe in herself and stay focused. All 110,000 people in the stadium were screaming; Go Cathy Go!

The noise in the stadium was enormous, everyone was standing up screaming and cheering for Cathy to win. Cathy had to stay focused and determined to pass all the other runners for her ultimate dream to become a reality. Before she knew it, Cathy had crossed the finish line first to win the gold medal! Cathy had finally achieved her dream that she had when she was just a little girl. At the end of the race, Cathy proudly draped the Aboriginal and Australian flags around her while she was cheered by the entire stadium.

Cathy once again had made history by being the first Aboriginal Australian to win an individual Olympic gold medal.

SYDNEY
Sydney 2000

When Cathy won the gold medal every kid in Australia wanted to be just like Cathy.

Cathy's win inspired us all that dreams really do come true and she proved to herself, and everyone else that if you truly believe in yourself and never give up; you too can be a champion just like Cathy.

FUN QUESTIONS

[1] Where was Cathy born?

[2] What did the sign say that Cathy put up in her house when she was a kid?

[3] What year was Cathy named Young Australian of the Year?

[4] Was Cathy the first female Aboriginal Australian to win a gold medal at the Commonwealth Games?

[5] What was Cathy's dream when she was a little girl?

[6] From 1996 until 2000 how many races did Cathy win?

[7] Besides winning a gold medal at the 2000 Sydney Olympic Games what else did Cathy do that was special?

[8] What were the 110,000 people in the stadium screaming while Cathy was running?

[9] What two flags did Cathy put around her after winning the gold medal?

[10] Cathy's dream when she was a kid was to win a gold medal at the Olympics, what is your dream?

ABOUT THE AUTHOR

Richard Simpkin was born in Sydney, Australia in 1973 and has worked as a photographer in Australia, England and the US for 25 years.

He is a best-selling author of five books, two of which are about Australian legends who he met, photographed and interviewed.

In 2014 Richard also founded World Letter Writing Day and has inspired children and adults all around the world to take a break from social media and write handwritten letters.

Richard has also conducted many workshops at schools in Australia. The students often ask him about many of the Australian legends that he has met over the years. This has inspired Richard to create these fun yet educational books about iconic Australians who we should all know about.

Other books by author

Australian Legends, 2005
Richard and Famous, 2007
100 Australian Legends, 2014
Michael in Pictures, 2015
Richard Simpkin Celebrity Quotes, 2016
Steve Irwin — Aussie Big Achievers, 2021
Ash Barty — Aussie Big Achievers, 2021
Shane Warne — Aussie Big Achievers, 2022

OTHER AUSSIE BIG ACHIEVERS BOOKS

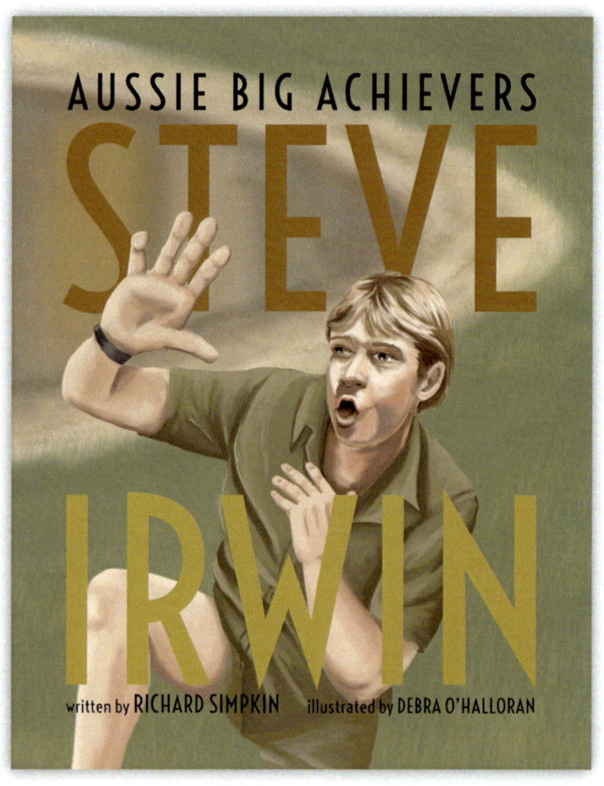

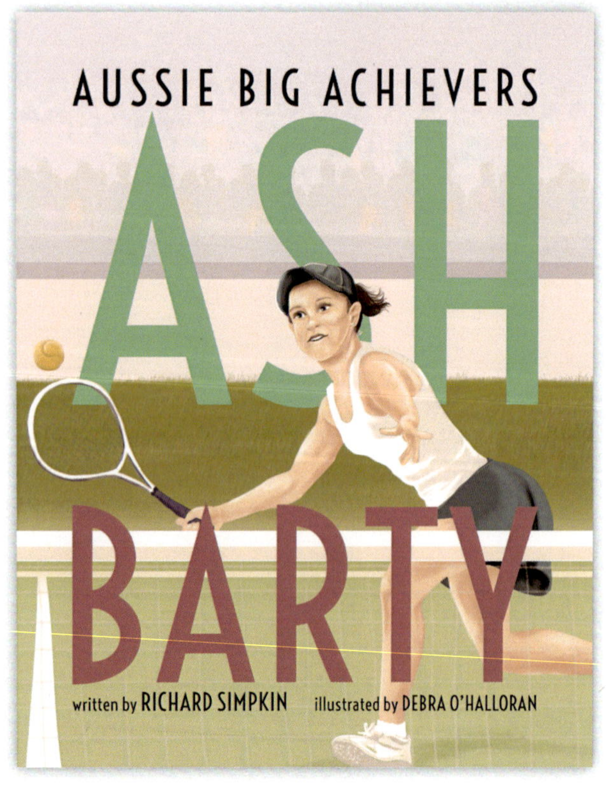

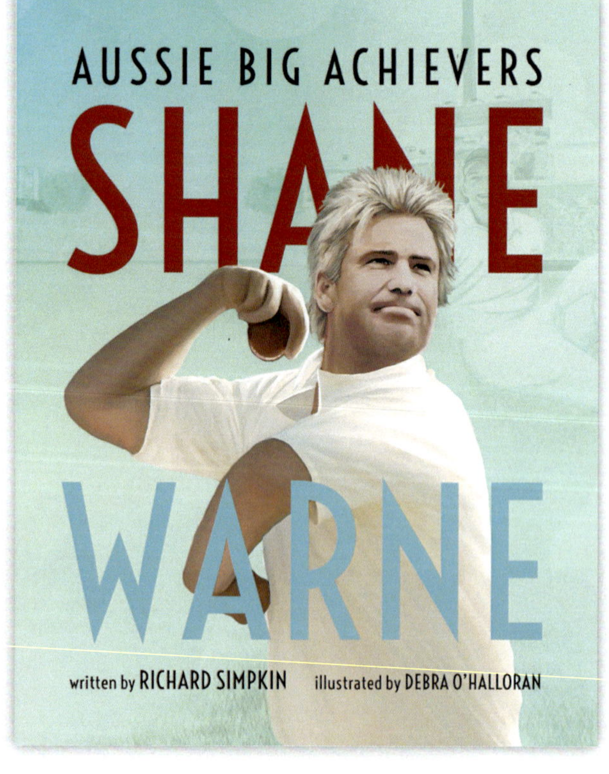